Peekaboo Baby
Où est le bébé

Sujatha Lalgudi

Author/Illustrator: Sujatha Lalgudi
Translator: Audrey Marcel

This book belongs to:

_ _

Where are the baby's eyes?

Où sont les yeux du bébé?

Here they are, two twinkling eyes.

Les voici, deux yeux qui font des clins d'oeil.

Where is the baby's nose?

Où est le nez du bébé?

Here it is, one shiny nose.

Le voici, un nez brillant.

Where is the baby's mouth?

Où est la bouche du bébé?

Here it is, rosy lips.

Les voici, des lèvres roses.

Where are the baby's ears?

Où sont les oreilles du bébé?

Here they are, two ears that hear.

Les voici, deux oreilles qui entendent.

Where are the baby's fingers?

Où sont les doigts du bébé?

Here they are, ten lovely fingers.

Les voici, dix jolis doigts.

Where are the baby's toes?

Où sont les orteils du bébé?

Here they are, ten tiny toes.

Les voici, dix orteils.

Where is the baby's belly button?

Où est le nombril du bébé ?

Here it is!

Le voici.

Where is the baby?

Où est le bébé?

Here I am!

Me voilà !

Peekaboo, baby.

Où est le bébé.

It is time to sleep baby.

Bébé, il est
temps de dormir.

Good Night.

Bonne nuit.

Sweet Dreams Baby!

Fais de beaux
rêves bébé.

If you enjoyed reading this book, please write a short review. It will help us spread the word. Thank you!

Si vous avez aimé ce livre,
écrivez-nous s'il vous plait un commentaire.
Cela nous aidera à promouvoir ce livre. Merci.

-Sujatha Lalgudi

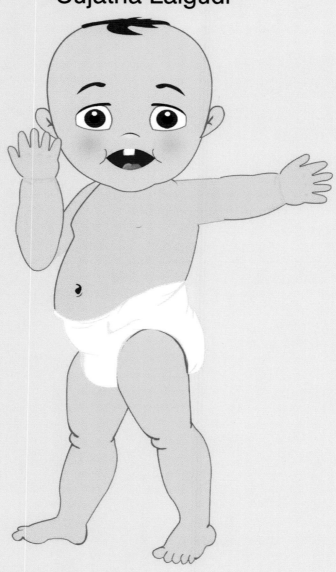

The End.

Lost in the Snow

by Claire Alexander

Albury Children's

For
Beautiful Mia

First published in 2010 by Gullane Children's Books

This edition published in 2014 by Albury Books,
Albury Court, Albury, Thame, OX9 2LP, United Kingdom

Text © Claire Alexander • Illustrations © Claire Alexander
The rights of Claire Alexander to be identified as the author and illustrator have been
asserted by them in accordance with the Copyright, Designs
and Patents Act, 1988

For orders: Kuperard Publishers and Distributors +44 (0) 208 4462440

ISBN 978-1-910235-64-5 (paperback)

A CIP catalogue record for this book is available from the British Library
10 9 8 7 6 5 4 3
Printed in China

Lost in the Snow

by Claire Alexander

One day in winter,
two fox cubs watched the
snowfall for the first time.

Mother Fox said,
"You can go out and play,
as long as you stay
where I can see you."

Benny was the first to leave the den.
He was so excited, he jumped head-first into the snow.

Fern followed a little more carefully. First she peeped out . . .

then she sniffed the snow . . .

and then she tested it with her paw.
Finally she was ready to venture out.

Fern made lots of lovely neat tracks in the snow,
while Benny kicked it up all over the place.
"This is so much fun!" he cried.

Just then, they heard a noise in the distance –
a **swoosh** and **wheee!**
coming from over the hill.

"What's that?" asked Fern.
"Let's go and see!" said Benny.

"Mummy said to stay close,"
said Fern.

But Benny was already
too far away to hear her.

"Come back, Benny!" Fern cried.

But Benny kept going, further and further . . .

and further until . . .

"Look!" cried Benny . . .

"Ice-skating hares!"

It looked so much fun, Fern forgot to tell
Benny that Mummy might be worried.

And when Benny raced down the hill . . .   Fern followed.

"Hello! Come and join us," called the hares.
"We'll teach you to skate!"

Soon Fern and Benny were
whizzing about on the ice.
"Wheeeeee!" cried Benny.
"This is so much fun!" laughed Fern.

Eventually the sun started to go down.
It was time for the hares to go home.
"We should go home too, Benny," said Fern, as she
remembered what their mummy had said to them.

So they raced back up the hill.
"Which way now?" asked Fern.

Benny didn't know.
"WE ARE LOST!" he cried.

Benny was scared.

Fern was scared too.

But then something caught her eye. . .

"I remember that pretty flower!" said Fern. "This is the way home!"

"Come on, Benny – follow me!" she called. "Mind your head . . .

and watch out for the tree stump!"

And before they knew it, there was . . .

Mummy!

"You naughty little cubs, where have you been?" she
scolded. "I was so worried about you!"

"We're sorry, Mummy,"
said Fern and Benny.
"We'll never run away again."

"I'm just so pleased to have you back,"
said Mummy, as she hugged her
little cubs tightly to her.

After that Benny was a little more sensible,
and Fern was a little less timid. And both of them
had lots more fun in the snow!